The Masque of Blacknesse

The Masque of Beauty

BY

BEN JONSON

CHARACTERS

of

Two royall Masques.

The one of BLACKNESSE,
The other of BEAVTIE.

personated

By the most magnificent of Queenes

ANNE

Queene of great Britaine, ^{&c.}

With her honorable Ladyes,

1605. *and* 1608.

at White-Hall:

and

Inuented by B E N: I O N S O N.

Ouid. —*Salue festa dies, meliorque reuertere semper.*

Contents

The Masque of Blacknesse

THE

QVEENES
MASQVES.

The first, of Blacknesse: *personated at the*
Court, at WHITE-HALL, *on the*
Twelu'th night.
1605.

He honor; and splendor of these S*pectacles* was such in the performance, as could those houres haue lasted, this of mine, now; had beene a most vnprofitable worke. But (when it is the fate, euen of the greatest, and most absolute births, to need, and borrow a life of posterity) little had beene done to the study of *magnificence* in these; if presently with the rage of the people, who (as a part of greatnesse) are priuiledged by Custome, to deface their *carkasses*, the *spirits* had also perished. In dutie, therefore, to that *Maiestie*, who gaue them their authoritie, and grace; and, no lesse then the most royall of predecessors, deserues eminent celebration for these solemnities: I adde this later hand, to redeeme them as well from ignorance, as enuie, two common euills, the one of *Censure*, the other of *Obliuion.*

P LINIE, S OLINVS, P TOLEMAEE, and of late LEO the *African*, remember vnto vs a riuer in *Æthiopia*, famous by the name of *Niger*; of which the people were called *Negritœ*, now *Negro*'s: and are the blackest nation of the world. This riuer taketh spring out of a certaine *Lake*, east-ward; & after a long race, falleth into the westerne *Ocean*. Hence (because it was her Maiesties will, to haue them *Black-mores* at first) the inuention was deriued by me, & presented thus.

First, for the *Scene*, was drawne a *Landtschape*, consisting of small woods, and here and there a voide place filld with huntings; which falling, an artificiall Sea was seene to shoote forth, as if it flowed to the land, raised with waues, which seemed to moue, and in some places the billow to breake, as imitating that orderly disorder, which is common in nature. In front of this Sea were placed sixe *Tritons*, in mouing, and sprightly actions, their vpper parts humane, saue that their haires were blue, as partaking of the Sea-colour: their desinent parts, fishe, mounted aboue their heads, and all varied in disposition. From their backs were borne out certaine light pieces of Taffata, as if carried by the winde, and their Musique made out of wreathed shells. Behinde these, a paire of *Sea-Maides*, for song, were as conspicuously seated; betweene which, two great Sea-horses (as bigge as the life) put forth themselues; the one mounting aloft, & writhing his head from the other, which seemed to sinck forwards; so intended for variation, & that the Figure behind, might come off better: vpon their backs, OCEANVS & NIGER were aduanced.

OCEANVS, presented in a humane forme; the colour of his flesh, blew; and shadowed with a robe of Sea-greene; his head grey; & horned; as he is described by the *Antients*: his beard of the like mixt colour: hee was gyrlonded with *Alga*, or Sea-grasse; and in his hand a *Trident*.

NIGER, in forme and colour of an *Æthiope*; his haire, and rare beard curled, shadowed with a blue, and bright mantle: his front, neck, and wrists adorned with Pearle, and crowned, with an artificiall wreathe of Cane, and Paper-rush.

These induced the *Masquers*, which were twelue *Nymphs*, *Negro*'s; and the daughters of NIGER; attended by so many of the OCEANAE, which were their *Light-bearers*.

The *Masquers* were placed in a great concaue shell, like mother of Pearle, curiously made to moue on those waters, and rise with the billow; the top thereof was stuck with a *cheu'ron* of lights, which, indented to the proportion of the shell, strooke a glorious beame vpon them, as they were seated, one aboue another: so that they were all seene, but in an extravagant order.
On sides of the shell, did swim six huge *Sea-monsters*, varied in their shapes, and dispositions, bearing on their backs the twelue *Torch bearers*; who were planted there in seuerall graces; so as the backs of some were seene; some in *purfle*, or side; others in face; & all hauing their lights burning out of W*helks*, or M*u-rex* shels.

The attire of the *Masquers* was alike, in all, without difference: the colours, *Azure*, and *Siluer*; their hayre thicke, and curled vpright in tresses, lyke *Pyramids*, but returned on the top with a scrole and antique dressing of Feathers, and Iewels inter-laced with ropes of Pearle. And, for the front, eare, neck, and wrists, the ornament was of the most choise and orient Pearle; best setting

For the *Light bearers, Sea-greene*, waued about the skirts with gold and siluer; their hayre loose, and flowing, gyr-landed with Sea-grasse, and that stuck with branches of Corall.

BEN JONSON

These thus presented, the *Scene* behind, seemed a vast Sea (and vnited with this that flowed forth) from the termination, or *horizon* of which (being the leuell of the *State*, which was placed in the vpper end of the Hall) was drawne, by the lines of *Prospectiue*, the whole worke shooting downe-wards, from the eye; which *decorum* made it more conspicuous, and caught the eye a farre off with a wandring beauty. To which was added an obscure and cloudy night-piece, that made the whole set off. So much for the bodily part. Which was of master YNIG O IONES his designe, and act.

By this, one of the *Tritons*, with the two *Sea-Maides*, began to sing to the others lowd Musique, their voyces being a *tenor*, and two *trebles*.

S O N G.

Sound, sound aloud
The welcome of the orient *Floud,*
Into the West;

Fayre, N IGE R, *sonne to great* O CEANV S,
Now honord, thus,
With all his beauteous race:
Who, though but blacke in face,
Yet, are they bright,
And full of life, and light.
To proue that Beauty best,
Which not the colour, but the feature
Assures vnto the creature.

O C E A N V S.

Be silent, now the Ceremonies done,
And N IGE R, *say, how comes it, louely Sonne,*
That thou, the Æ THIOPES *Riuer, so farre* East,
Art seene to fall into the'extreamest West
Of me, the King of flouds, O CEANV S,
And, in mine Empires heart, salute me thus?
My ceaselesse current, now, amazed stands!
To see thy labor, through so many lands,
 Mix thy fresh billow, with my brackish streame;
And, in thy sweetnesse, stretch thy diademe,

BEN JONSON

To these farre distant, and vn-equall'd skies
This squared Circle of cœlestiall bodies.

N I G E R.

Diuine O ceanvs, *tis not strange at all,*
That (since the immortall soules of creatures mortal,
Mixe with their bodies, yet reserue for euer
A powre of seperation) I should seuer
My fresh streames, from thy brackish (like things fixed)
Though, with thy powerfull saltnes, thus far mixed.
"Vertue, though chain'd to earth, will still liue free;
"And Hell it selfe must yeeld to industry.

O C E A N V S.

Bvt, what's the end of thy Herculean *labors,*
Extended to these calme, and blessed shores?

NIGER.

To do a kind, and carefull Fathers part,
In satisfying euery pensiue heart
Of these my Daughters, *my most loued birth:*

8

MASQUE OF BLACKNESS

Who though they were the first form'd Dames of earth,
And in whose sparckling, and refulgent eyes,
The glorious Sunne *did still delight to rise;*
Though he (the best Iudge, and most formall cause
Of all Dames beauties) in their firm hiewes, drawes
Signes of his feruent'st Loue; and thereby shewes
That, in their black, the perfectst beauty growes;
Since the fix't colour of their curled haire,
(Which is the highest grace of dames most faire)
No cares, no age can change; or there display
The fearefull tincture of abhorred Gray;
Since Death *hir selfe (hir selfe being pale & blue)*
Can neuer alter their most faith-full hew;
All which are arguments, to proue, how far
Their beauties conquer, in great Beauties warre;
And more, how neere Diuinity *they be,*
That stand from passion, or decay so free.
Yet, since the fabulous voices of some few
Poore brain-sicke men, stil'd Poets, *here with you,*
Haue, with such enuy of their graces, sung
The painted Beauties, *other* Empires *sprung;*
Letting their loose, and winged fictions fly
To infect all clymates, yea our purity;

As of one P HAETON, *that fir'd the world,*
And, that, before his heedles flames were hurld
About the Globe, *the* Æthiopes *were as faire,*
As other Dames; *now blacke, with blacke dispaire:*
And in respect of their complections chang'd,
Are each where, since, for lucklesse creatures rang'd.
Which, when my Daughters *heard, (as women are*
Most iealous of their beauties) feare, and care
Possess'd them whole; yea, and beleeuing them,
They wept such ceaseles teares, into my streame,

9

That it hath, thus far, ouerflow'd his shore
To seeke them patience: who haue since, ere more
As the Sunne *riseth, charg'd his burning throne*
With volleys of reuilings; 'cause he shone
On their scorch'd cheekes, with such intemperate fires,
And other Dames, *made Queenes of all desires.*
To frustrate which strange error, oft, I sought,
(Though most in vaine, against a setled thought
As women are) till they confirm'd at length
By miracle, what I, with so much strength
Of argument resisted; els they fain'd:
For in the Lake, *where their first spring they gain'd,*
As they sate, cooling their soft Limmes, one night,
Appear'd a Face, all circumfus'd with light;
(And sure they saw't, for Æthiopes neuer dreame)
Wherein they might decipher through the streame,
These words.

That they a *Land* must forthwith seeke,
Whose termination (of the *Greeke*)
Sounds T A N I A; where bright *Sol*, that heat

.

Their blouds, doth neuer rise, or set,
But in his Iourney passeth by,
And leaues that *Clymat* of the sky,
To comfort of a greater *Light*,
Who formes all beauty, with his sight.

In search of this, haue we three Princedomes *past,*
That speake out Tania, *in their accents last;*
Blacke Mauritania, *first; and secondly,*
Swarth Lusitania; *next, we did descry*
Rich Aquitania; *and, yet, cannot find*
The place vnto these longing Nymphes design'd.

Instruct, and ayde me, great O C E A N V S,
What land is this, that now appeares to vs?

OCEANVS.

This Land, t*hat lifts into the temperate ayre*

His snowy cliffe, is Albion *the faire;*
So call'd of Neptunes son, who ruleth here:
For whose deare guard, my selfe, (foure thousand yeere,
Since old Deucalion's *daies) haue walk'd the round*
About his empire, proud, to see him crown'd
Aboue my waues.

At this, the *Moone* was discouered in the vpper part of the
house, triumphant in a *Siluer* throne, made in figure of a
Pyramis. Her garments *White*, and *Siluer*, the dressing of her
head antique; & crown'd with a *Luminarie*, or *Sphære* of light:
which striking on the clouds, and heightened with *Siluer*, reflected as naturall clouds doe by the splendour of the *Moone*.
The heauen, about her, was vaulted with blew silke, and set with
Starres of *Siluer* which had in them their seuerall lights burning.
The suddaine sight of which, made NIGER to interrupt O C E A N V S,
with this present passion.

N I G E R.

—O see, our siluer Starre!
Whose pure, auspicious light greetes vs, thus farre!

11

BEN JONSON

Great Æthiopia, Goddesse of our shore,
Since, with particular worshippe we adore
Thy generall brightnesse, let particular grace
Shyne on my zealous Daughters: *Shew the place,*
Which, long, their longings vrg'd their eyes to see.
Beautifie them, which long haue Deified thee.

ÆTHIOPIA.

Niger, be glad: Resume thy natiue cheare.
Thy Daughters labors haue their period here,
And so thy errors. I was that bright Face
Reflected by the Lake, *in which thy* Race
Read mysticke lines; (which skill PITHAGORAS
First taught to men, by a reuerberate glasse)
This blessed Isle doth with that TANIA *end,*
Which there they saw inscrib'd, and shall extend
Wish'd satisfaction to their best desires.
BRITANIA, *which the triple world admires,*
This Isle hath now recouered for her name;
Where raigne those Beauties, that with so much fame
The sacred MVSES *Sonnes haue honored,*
And from bright HESPERVS *to* EOVS *spred.*
With that great name BRITANIA, *this blest Isle*
Hath wonne her ancient dignitie, and stile,
A World, diuided from the world: *and tri'd*
The abstract of it, in his generall pride.
For were the world, with all his wealth, a Ring,
BRITANIA *(whose new name makes all tongues sing)*
Might be a Diamant worthy to inchase it,
Rul'd by a SVNNE, *that to this height doth grace it:*
Whose Beames shine day, and night, and are of force

12

To blanch an Æ THIOPE, *and reuiue a* Cor's.
His light scientiall is, and (past mere nature)
Can salue the rude defects of euery creature.
　　Call forth thy honor'd Daughters, *then;*
　　And let them, 'fore the Brittaine *men,*
　　Indent the Land, *with those pure traces*
　　They flow with, in their natiue graces.
　　Inuite them, boldly, to the shore,
　　Their Beauties shalbe scorch'd no more:
　　This Sunne *is temperate, and refines*
　　All things, on which his radiance shines.

　　　　Here the *Tritons* sounded, & they daunced on shore, euery couple (as they aduanced) seuerally presenting their Fans: in one of which were inscribed their mixt *Names*, in the other a mute *Hieroglyphick*, expressing their mixed quallities. Which manner of *Symbole* I rather chose, then *Imprese*, as well for strangenesse, as relishing of antiquity, and more applying to that originall doctrine of sculpture, which the *Ægyptians* are said, first, to haue brought from the *Æthiopians.*

BEN JONSON

	The Names.	*The Symboles.*
The Queene.	1. {E V P H O R I S.	1.{A golden Tree, la-
Co: of Bedford.	{A G L A I A.	{den with fruict.
La: Herbert.	2. {D I A P H A N E.	2. {The figure *Icosae-*
Co: of Derby	{E V C A M P S E.	{*dron* of crystall.
La: Rich.	3. {O C Y T E.	3. {A payre of naked
Co: of Suffolke.	{K A T H A R E.	{feet, in a Riuer.
La: Beuill.	4. {N O T I S.	4. {The Salaman-
La: Effingham.	{P S Y C H R O T E.	{der simple.
La: El. Howard.	5. {G L Y C Y T E.	5. {A clowd full of
La: Sus: Vere.	{M A L A C I A.	{raine, dropping.
La: Wroth.	6. {B A R Y T E.	6. {An vrne[,] spheared
La: Walsingham	{P E R I P H E R E.	{with wine.

The names of the O C E A N I A E were.

DORIS.   CYDIPPE.   BEROE.   IANTHE.

PETRAEA.   GLAVCE.   ACASTE.   LYCORIS.

OCYRHOE.   TYCHE.   CLYTIA.   PLEXAVRE.

Their owne single *Daunce* ended, as they were about to
make choice of their Men: One, from the Sea, was heard to call
'hem with this *charme*, sung by a *tenor* voyce.

S O N G.

Come away, come away,
We grow iealous of your stay:
If you do not stop your eare,
We shall haue more cause to feare
Syrens *of the land, then they*
To doubt the Syrens *of the Sea.*

Here they daunc'd with their men, seuerall *measures*, and
corranto's. All which ended, they were againe accited to sea,
with a *Song* of two *Trebles*, whose cadences were iterated by a
double *Eccho*, from seuerall parts of the Land.

S O N G.

Daughters of the subtle Flood,
Doe not let Earth longer intertayne you;
   1. Ecch. { *Let Earth longer intertaine you.*
    2. Ecch. { *Longer intertaine you.*

15

'Tis to them, inough of good,
That you giue this little hope, to gaine you.
   1. Ecch. { *Giue this little hope, to gaine you.*
    2. Ecch. *Little hope, to gaine you.*

If they loue,
   You shall quickly see;
 For when to flight you mooue,
They'll follow you, the more you flee.
   1. Ecch. { *Follow you, the more you flee.*
    2. Ecch. *The more you flee.*

 If not, impute it to each others matter;
They are but Earth, & what you vow'd was Water.

   1. Ecch. *And what you vow'd*
was Water.
    2. Ecch. *You vow'd was*
Water.

AETHIOPIA.

 Inough, bright Nymphes, *the night growes old,*
And we are grieu'd, we can not hold
You longer light: But comfort take.
Your Father, *onely, to the* Lake
Shall make returne: Your selues, with feasts,
Must here remayne the Ocean's *guests.*
Nor shall this vayle, the Sunne *hath cast*
Aboue your bloud, more Summers last.
For which, you shall obserue these rites.
Thirteene times thrise, on thirteene nights,
(So often as I fill my Sphære

With glorious light, throughout the yeere)
You shall (when all things els do sleepe
Saue your chast thoughts) with reuerence, steepe
Your bodies in that purer brine,
And wholesome dew, call'd Ros-marine:
Then with that soft, and gentler fome,
Of which, the Ocean, *yet, yeelds some,*
Whereof bright V E N V S, *Beauties Queene,*
Is sayd to haue begotten beene,
You shall your gentler limmes ore-laue,
And for your paines, perfection haue.
So that this night, the yeare gone round,
You doe againe salute this ground;
And, in the beames of yond' bright Sunne,
Your faces dry, and all is done.

At which, in a *Daunce* they returned to the Sea, where they tooke their Shell; and, with this full *Song*, went out.

SONG.

Now Dian, *with her burning face,*
Declines apace:
By which our Waters know
To ebbe, that late did flow.
Back Seas, back Nymphes; *but, with a forward grace,*
Keepe, still, your reuerence to the place:
And shout with ioy of fauor, you haue wonne,
In sight of Albion, Neptunes *Sonne.*

So ended the first *Masque,* which (beside the singular grace of *Musicke* and *Daunces*) had that successe in the nobilitie of performance; as nothing needes to the illustration, but the memory by whome it was personated.

The Masque of Beauty

THE

SECOND

MASQVE.

Which was of Beauty; *was presented in the same Court, at* WHITE-HALL, *on the Sunday night, after the twelfth Night.*
1608.

Two yeares being now past, that her *Maiesty* had intermitted these delights, and the third almost come; it was her
Highnesse pleasure againe to glorifie the *Court*, & command
that I should thinke on some fit presentment, which should an-
swere the former, still keeping then the same persons, the
Daughters of N I G E R; but their beauties varied according to
promise, and their time of absence excus'd, with foure more
added to their Number.

To which limitts, when I had adapted my inuention, and
being to bring newes of them, from the Sea, I induc'd *Boreas*,
one of the windes, as my fitest Messenger; presenting him thus.

In a robe of *Russet*, and *White* mixt, full, and bagg'd: his
haire, and beard rough: and horrid; his wings gray, and ful of
snow, and icycles. His mantle borne from him with wires, & in
seuerall puffes; his feet   ending in serpents tayles; and in his
hand a leaueles *Branch*, laden with icycles

But before, in midst of the *Hall*; to keepe the State of the
feast, and season; I had placed *Ianuary*, in a throne of *Siluer*:
His robe of *Ash-collour*, long, fringed with *Siluer,* a white mantle. His winges white, and his buskins; in his hand a *Laurell*
bough, vpon his head an *Anademe* of *Laurell*, fronted with the
signe *Aquarius*, and the *Character*. Who as *Boreas* blusterd
forth, discouer'd himselfe

BEN JONSON

B O R E A S.

Which among these is Albion, Neptunes *Sonne?*

I A N V A R I V S.

What ignorance dares make that question?
Would any aske, who Mars *were in the wars?*
Or, which is Hesperus, *among the starres?*
Of the bright Planets, *which is* Sol? *Or can*
A doubt arise, 'mong creatures, which is man?
Behold, whose eyes do dart Promethian *fire*
Throughout this all; whose precepts do inspire
The rest with duty; yet commanding, cheare:
And are obeyed, more with loue, then feare.

B O R E A S.

What Power art thou, that thus informest me?

I A N V A R I V S.

Dost thou not know me? I, to well, know thee
By thy rude voyce, that doth so hoarely blow,

24

Thy haire, thy beard, thy wings, ore-hil'd with snow,
Thy Serpent feet, to be that rough North-winde,
Boreas, *that, to my raigne, art still vnkinde.*
I am the Prince of Months, call'd Ianuary;
Because by me Ianus *the yeare doth vary,*
Shutting vp warres, proclayming peace, & feasts,
Freedome, & triumphes: making Kings his guests.

B O R E A S.

To thee then, thus, & by thee, to that King,
That doth thee present honors, do I bring
Present remembrance of twelue Æthiope *Dames:*
Who; guided hither by the Moones *bright flames,*
To see his brighter light, were to the Sea
Enioyn'd againe, and (thence assign'd a day
for their returne) were in the waues to leaue
Theyr blacknesse, *and true* beauty *to receaue.*

I A N V A R I V S.

 Which they receau'd, but broke theyr day: & yet
Haue not return'd a looke of grace for it,
Shewing a course, and most vnfit neglect.
Twise haue I come, in pompe here, to expect
Theyr presence; Twise deluded, haue bene faine
With   other rites my Feasts to intertayne:
And, now the Third time, turn'd about the yeare
Since they were look'd for; and, yet, are not here.

BEN JONSON

B O R E A S.

It was nor Will, nor Sloth, that caus'd theyr stay,
For they were all prepared by theyr day,
And, with religion, forward on theyr way:
When PROTEVS, *the gray* Prophet *of the Sea Met them, and*
made report, how other foure
Of their blacke kind, (whereof theyr Sire had store)
Faithfull to that great wonder, so late done
Vpon theyr Sisters, by bright Albion,
Had followed them to seeke BRITANIA *forth,*
And there, to hope like fauor, as like worth.
Which Night envy'd, as done in her despight,
And (mad to see an Æthiope washed white,
Thought to preuent in these; least men should deeme
Her coulor, if thus chang'd; of small esteeme.
And so, by mallice, and her magicke, tost
The Nymphes *at Sea; as they were almost lost,*
Till, on a Iland, they by chance arriu'd,
That floted in the mayne, where, yet, she' had giu'd
Them so, in charmes of darknes, as no might
Should loose them thence, but theyr chang'd Sisters sight.
Whereat the Twelue *(in piety mou'd, & kind)*
Streight, put themselues in act, the place to finde;
Which was the Nights *sole trust they so will do,*
That she, with labor might confound them too.
For, euer since, with error hath she held
Them wandring in the Ocean, *and so quell'd*
Their hopes beneath their toyle, as (desperat now
Of any least successe vnto their vow;
Nor knowing to returne to expresse the grace,
Wherewith they labor to this Prince, and place)
One of them, meeting me at Sea, *did pray,*
That for the loue of my ORYTHIA,
(Whose very name did heate my frosty brest,
And make me shake my Snow fill'd wings, & crest)

To beare this sad report I would be wonne,
And frame their iust excuse: which here I haue done.

I A N V A R I V S.

Would thou hadst not begun, vnluckie Winde,
That neuer yet blew'st goodnes to mankind;
But with thy bitter, and too piercing breath,
Strik'st horrors through the ayre, as sharp as death.

Here a second Wind came in, *VVLTVRNVS*, in a *blew* coulored robe & mantle, pufft as the former, but somewhat sweeter, his face blacke, and on his head, a red *Sunne*, shewing he came from the East; his winges of seuerall coullors; his buskins *white*, and wrought with *Gold*.

VVLTVRNVS.

All horrors vanish, and all name of Death,
Bee all things here as calme as is my breath.
A gentler Wind, Vulturnus, *brings you newes*
The Ile *is found, & that the* Nymphs *now vse*
Their rest, & ioy. The Nights *black charmes are flowne.*
For, being made vnto their Goddesse *knowne,*
Bright Æthiopia, *the siluer* Moone,

As she was   Hecate, *she brake them soone:*
And now by vertue of their light, and grace,
The glorious Isle, *wherein they rest, takes place*
Of all the earth for Beauty.   There, their Queen
Hath raysed them a Throne, *that still is seene*
To turne vnto the motion of the World,
Wherein they sit, and are, like Heauen, whirld
About the Earth, whilst, to them contrary,
(Following those nobler torches of the Sky)
A world of little Loues, *and chast* Desires,
Do light their beauties, with still mouing fires.
And who to Heauens *consent can better moue,*
Then those that are so like it, Beauty *and* Loue?
Hether, as to theyr new Elysium,
The spirits of the antique Greekes *are come,*
Poets, *and* Singers, Linus, Orpheus, *all*
That haue excell'd in   knowledge musicall;
Where, set in Arbor made of myrtle, and gold,
They liue, againe, these Beautyes to behold.
And thence, in flowry mazes walking forth
Sing hymnes in celebration of their worth.
Whilst, to theyr Songs, two Fountaynes flow, one hight
Of lasting Youth, *the other chast* Delight,
That at the closes, from theyr bottomes spring,
And strike the Ayre to eccho *what they sing.*
But, why do I describe what all must see?
By this time, nere thy coast, they floating be;
For, so their vertuous Goddesse, *the chast* Moone,
*Told them, the Fate of th'*Iland *should, & soone*
Would fixe it selfe vnto thy continent,
As being the place, by Destiny fore-ment,
Where they should flow forth, drest in her attyres:
And, that the influence of those holy fires,
(First rapt from hence) being multiplied vpon
The other foure, *should make their Beauties one.*

Which now expect to see, great Neptunes *Sonne,*
And loue the miracle, which thy selfe hast done.

Here, a Curtine was drawne (in which the *Night* was painted.) and the *Scene* discouer'd. which (because the former was *marine*, and these, yet of necessity, to come from the Sea) I deuisd, should bee an *Island*, floting on a calme water. In the middst therof was a Seate of state, cal'd the *Throne* of *Beautie*, erected: diuided into eight *Squares*, and distinguish'd by so many *Ionick piliasters*. In these *Squares* the sixteene *Masquers* were plac'd by couples: behind them, in the center of the *Throne* was a tralucent *Pillar*, shining with seuerall colour'd lights, that reflected on their backs. From the top of which *Pillar* went seuerall arches to the *Pilasters*, that sustained the roofe of the *Throne*, which was likewise adorn'd with lights, and gyrlonds; And betweene the *Pilasters*, in front, little *Cupids* in flying posture, wauing of wreaths; and lights, bore vp the *Coronice*: ouer which were placed eight *Figures*, representing the *Elements* of *Beauty*; which aduanced vpon the *Ionick*; and being *females*, had the Corinthian order. The first was

S P L E N D O R.

In a robe of *flame* colour, naked brested; her bright hayre loose flowing: She was drawne in a circle of clowdes, her face, and body breaking through; and in her hand a branch, with two *Roses*, a *white*, and a *red*. The next to her was

S E R E N I T A S.

In a garment of bright *skye* colour, a long tresse, & waued with a vayle of diuers colours, such as the golden skie sometimes shewes: vpon her head a cleare, and faire *Sunne* shining, with rayes of gold striking downe to the feete of the figure. In her hand a *Christall*, cut with seuerall angles, and shadow'd with diuerse colours, as causd by refraction. The third

BEN JONSON

GERMINATIO.

In greene; with a *Zone* of golde about her Wast, crowned with
Myrtle, her haire likewise flowing, but not of so bright a colour:
In her hand, a branch of *Myrtle*. Her socks of greene, and *Gold*.
The fourth was

LAETITIA.

In a Vesture of diuerse colours, and all sorts of flowers embroi-
dered thereon. Her socks so fitted. A *Gyrland* of flowers in her
hand; her eyes turning vp, and smiling, her haire flowing, and
stuck with flowers.   The fift

TEMPERIES.

In a garment of *Gold*, *Siluer*, and colours weaued: In one hand
shee held a   burning

Steele, in the other, an *Vrne* with water. On her head a gyrland
of flowers, Corne, Vine-leaues, and Oliue branches, enter-
wouen. Her socks, as her garment.   The sixth

VENVSTAS.

In a Siluer robe, with a thinne subtle vaile ouer her haire, and it:
Pearle about her neck, and forhead. Her socks wrought with
pearle. In her hand shee bore seuerall colour'd *Lillies*.   The
seauenth was

DIGNITAS.

In a dressing of State, the haire bound vp with fillets of gold, the Garments rich, and set with iewells, and gold; likewise her buskins, and in her hand a *Golden rod.*   The eight

PERFECTIO.

In a Vesture of pure *Gold,* a wreath of *Gold* vpon her head. About her body the *Zodiack,* with the *Signes*: In her hand a *Compasse* of gold, drawing a *circle.*

On the top of all the *Throne,* (as being made out of all these) stood

HARMONIA.

A Personage, whose dressing had something of al the others, & had her robe painted full of *Figures.* Her head was compass'd with a crowne of *Gold,* hauing in it   seauen iewells equally set. In her hand a *Lyra,* wheron she rested.

This was the Ornament of the *Throne.* The ascent to which, consisting of sixe steppes, was couered with a   multitude of *Cupids* (chosen out of the best, and most ingenuous youth of the *Kingdome,* noble, and others) that were the *Torch-bearers*; and All armed, with *Bowes, Quiuers, Winges,* and other *Ensignes* of *Loue.* On the sides of the *Throne,* were curious, and elegant *Arbors* appointed: & behind, in the back part of the *Ile,* a *Groue,* of growne trees: laden with golden fruict, which other little *Cupids* plucked, and threw each at other, whilst on the ground *Leuerets* pick'd vp the bruised apples, and left them halfe eaten. The

31

BEN JONSON

Ground-plat of the whole was a subtle indented *Maze*; And, in the two formost angles, were two *Fountaines*, that ranne continually, the one *Hebes*, the other *Hedone*'s: In the *Arbors*, were plac'd the *Musitians*, who represented the *Shades* of the old *Poets*, & were attir'd in a *Priest*-like habit of *Crimson*, and *Purple*, with *Laurell* gyrlonds

The colours of the *Masquers* were varied; the one halfe in *Orange-tawny*, and *Siluer*: the other in *Sea-greene*, and *Siluer*. The bodies and short skirts of *White*, and *Gold*, to both.

The habite, and dressing (for the fashion) was most curious, and so exceeding in riches, as the *Throne* wheron they sat, seem'd to be a Mine of light, stroake from their iewells, & their garments

This *Throne*, (as the whole *Iland* mou'd onward, on the water,) had a circular motion of its owne, imitating that which we cal *Motum mundi*, from the *East* to the *West*, or the right to the left side. For so *Hom. Ilia. M.* vnderstands by *Orientalia mundi:* by ἀριστερὰ, *Occidentalia*. The steps, wheron the *Cupids* sate, had a motion contrary, with *Analogy, admotum Planetarum,* from the *West* to the *East*: both which turned with their seuerall lights. And with these three varied

Aboue which, the *Moone* was seene in a *Siluer* Chariot, drawne by *Virgins*, to ride in the cloudes, and hold them greater light: with the *Signe Scorpio*, and the *Character*, plac'd before her.

The order of this *Scene* was carefully, and ingeniously dispos'd; and as happily put in act for the *Motions*) by the *Kings* master Carpenter. The Paynters, I must needes say, (not to belie them) lent small colour to any, to attribute much of the spirit of these things to their pen'cills. But that must not bee imputed a crime either to the inuention, or designe

Here the loud *Musique* ceas'd; and the *Musitians*, which were placed in the *Arbors*, came forth through the *Mazes,* to the other Land: singing in this full *Song*, iterated in the closes by two *Eccho*'s, rising out of the Fountaines.

S O N G.

Wh*en* Loue, *at first, did mooue*
From out of Chaos, *brightned.*
So was the world, and lightned,
As now! Ecch. *As now!* Ecch. *As now!*
Yeeld Night, *then, to the light,*
As Blacknesse *hath to* Beauty:
Which is but the same duety.
It was for Beauty, *that the World was made,*
And where she raignes, Loues *lights admit no shade.*
Ecch. *Loues lights admit no shade.*
Ecch. *Admit no shade.*

Which ended, *Vulturnus* the Wind, spake to the Riuer *Thamesis* that lay along betweene the shores, leaning vpon his Vrne (that flow'd with water,) and crown'd with flowers; with a blew cloth of *Siluer* robe about him: and was personated by Maister THOMAS GILES, who made the *Daunces*.

BEN JONSON

VVLTVRNVS.

Rise aged Thames, *and by the hand*
Receiue these Nymphes, *within the land:*
And, in those curious Squares, *and* Rounds,
Wherewith thou flow'st betwixt the grounds,
Of fruictfull Kent, *and* Essex *faire,*
That lend thee gyrlands for thy haire;
Instruct their siluer feete to tread,
Whilst we, againe to sea, are fled.

   With which the *Windes* departed; and the *Riuer* receiu'd them
into the *Land,* by *couples & foures,* their *Cupids* comming before them.

Their persons were,

The QVEENE.	*La.* ANNE WINTER.
La. ARABELLA.	*La.* WINSORE.
Co. of ARVNDEL.	*La.* ANNE CLIFFORD.
Co. of DERBY.	*La.* MARY NEVILL.
Co. of BEDFORD.	*La.* ELIZ. HATTON.
Co. of MONTGOMERY.	*La.* ELIZ. GARRARD.
La. ELIZ. GILFORD.	*La.* CHICHESTER.
La. KAT. PETER.	*La.* WALSINGHAM.

   These dancing forth a most curious *Daunce,* full of excellent
deuice, and change, ended it in the figure of a *Diamant*, and so,
standing still, were by the *Musitians* with a second *Song* (sung
by a loud *Tenor*) celebrated.

So Beauty *on the waters stood,*
(*When* Loue *had seuer'd earth, from flood!*
So when he parted ayre, from fire,
He did with concord all inspire!
And then a Motion *he them taught,*
That elder than himselfe was thought.
Which thought was, yet, the child of earth,
For Loue *is elder then his birth.*

The *Song* ended; they *Daunced* forth their second *Daunce,*
more subtle, and full of change, then the former; and so exqui-
sitely performed, as the King's *Maiestie* incited first (by his
owne liking, to that which all others there present, wish'd) re-
quir'd them both againe, after some time of dauncing with the
Lords. Which time, to giue them respite, was intermitted with a
Song; first, by a *treble* voyce, in this manner.

If all these Cupids, *now, were blind*
As is their wanton Brother;
Or play should put it in their mind
To shoot at one another:
What pretty battayle they would make
If they their objects should mistake
And each one wound his Mother!

Which was seconded by another *treble*; thus.

It was no policy of Court,
Albee' the place were charmed,
To let in earnest, or in sport,
So many Loues *in, armed.*
For say, the Dames *should with their eyes,*

BEN JONSON

Vpon the hearts, here, mean surprize,
  Were not the men like harmed?

To which a *tenor* answered.

 Yes, were the Loues *or false, or straying;*
Or Beauties *not their beauty weighing:*
But here no such deceit is mix'd,
Their flames are pure, their eyes are fix'd:
They do not warre, with different darts,
But strike a musique of like hearts.

After which *Songs*, they danc'd *Galliards* and *Corranto*'s; and with those excellent *Graces*, that the Musique, appointed to celebrate them, shew'd it could be silent no longer: but, by the first *Tenor*, admir'd them thus:

S O N G.

 Had those, that dwelt in error foul
And hold that women haue no soule,
But seene these moue; they would haue, then
Sayd, Women were the souls of Men.
 So they do moue each heart, and eye,
  With the Worlds *soule, true Harmonie.*

Here, they daunc'd a third most elegant and curious *Daunce*, and not to be describ'd againe, by any art, but that of their own foot-

36

ing: which ending in the figure, that was to produce the fourth; *January* from his state saluted them, thus,

IANVARIVS.

 Your grace is great, as is your Beauty, Dames;
Inough my Feasts *haue prou'd your thankfull flames.*
Now vse your Seate: that seate which was, before,
Thought stray'ing, vncertayne, floting to each shore,
And to whose hauing euery Clime *laid clayme,*
Each Land, *and* Nation *vrged as the ayme*
Of their ambition, Beauties *perfect throne,*
Now made peculiar, to this place, alone;
And that, by'impulsion of your destinies,
And his attractiue beames, that lights these Skies:
*Who (though with th'*Ocean *compass'd) neuer wets*
His hayre therein, nor weares a beame that sets.
 Long may his light adorne these happy rites,
As I renew them; and your gratious sights
Enioy that happinesse, eu'en to enuy, as when
Beauty, *at large, brake forth, and conquer'd men.*

At which, they daunc'd theyr last *daunce,* into their *Throne againe: and that turning, the Scene* clos'd with this full *Song.*

S O N G.

 Still turne, and imitate the Heauen
   In motion swift and euen;
   And as his Planets *goe,*

Your brighter lights doe so:
May Youth *and* Pleasure *euer flow.*
    But let your State, the while,
    Be fixed as the Isle.
Cho. *{So all that see your* Beauties *sphære,*
    {May know the Elysian *fields are here.*
Echo. *{Th'Elysian fields are here.*
  Echo. *{Elysian fields are here.*

Also from Benediction Books ...

Wandering Between Two Worlds: Essays on Faith and Art
Anita Mathias
Benediction Books, 2007
152 pages
ISBN: 0955373700

Available from www.amazon.com, www.amazon.co.uk
www.wanderingbetweentwoworlds.com

In these wide-ranging lyrical essays, Anita Mathias writes, in lush, lovely prose, of her naughty Catholic childhood in Jamshedpur, India; her large, eccentric family in Mangalore, a sea-coast town converted by the Portuguese in the sixteenth century; her rebellion and atheism as a teenager in her Himalayan boarding school, run by German missionary nuns, St. Mary's Convent, Nainital; and her abrupt religious conversion after which she entered Mother Teresa's convent in Calcutta as a novice. Later rich, elegant essays explore the dualities of her life as a writer, mother, and Christian in the United States-- Domesticity and Art, Writing and Prayer, and the experience of being "an alien and stranger" as an immigrant in America, sensing the need for roots.

About the Author

Anita Mathias was born in India, has a B.A. and M.A. in English from Somerville College, Oxford University and an M.A. in Creative Writing from the Ohio State University. Her essays have been published in The Washington Post, The London Magazine, The Virginia Quarterly Review, Commonweal, Notre Dame Magazine, America, The Christian Century, Religion Online, The Southwest Review, Contemporary Literary Criticism, New Letters, The Journal, and two of HarperSanFrancisco's The Best Spiritual Writing anthologies. Her non-fiction has won fellowships from The National Endowment for the Arts; The Minnesota State Arts Board; The Jerome Foundation, The Vermont Studio Center; The Virginia Centre for the Creative Arts, and the First Prize for the Best General Interest Article from the Catholic Press Association of the United States and Canada. Anita has taught Creative Writing at the College of William and Mary, and now lives and writes in Oxford, England.

"Yesterday's Treasures for Today's Readers"

Titles by Benediction Classics available from Amazon.co.uk

Religio Medici, Hydriotaphia, Letter to a Friend, Thomas Browne

Pseudodoxia Epidemica: Or, Enquiries into Commonly Presumed Truths, Thomas Browne

The Maid's Tragedy, Beaumont and Fletcher

The Custom of the Country, Beaumont and Fletcher

Philaster Or Love Lies a Bleeding, Beaumont and Fletcher

A Treatise of Fishing with an Angle,   Dame Juliana Berners.

Pamphilia to Amphilanthus, Lady Mary Wroth

The Compleat Angler, Izaak Walton

The Magnetic Lady, Ben Jonson

Every Man Out of His Humour, Ben Jonson

The Masque of Blacknesse. The Masque of Beauty,. Ben Jonson

The Life of St. Thomas More, William Roper

Pendennis, William Makepeace Thackeray

Salmacis and Hermaphroditus attributed to Francis Beaumont

Friar Bacon and Friar Bungay Robert Greene

Holy Wisdom, Augustine Baker

The Jew of Malta and the Massacre at Paris, Christopher Marlowe

Tamburlaine the Great, Parts 1 & 2 AND Massacre at Paris, Christopher Marlowe

All Ovids Elegies, Lucans First Booke, Dido Queene of Carthage, Hero and Leander, Christopher Marlowe

The Titan, Theodore Dreiser

Scapegoats of the Empire: The true story of the Bushveldt Carbineers, George Witton

All Hallows' Eve, Charles Williams

Descent into Hell, Charles Williams

My Apprenticeship: Volumes I and II, Beatrice Webb

Last and First Men / Star Maker, Olaf Stapledon

Darkness and the Light, Olaf Stapledon

The Worst Journey in the World, Apsley Cherry-Garrard

The Schoole of Abuse, Containing a Pleasaunt Invective Against Poets, Pipers, Plaiers, Iesters and Such Like Catepillers of the Commonwelth, Stephen Gosson

Russia in the Shadows, H. G. Wells

Wild Swans at Coole, W. B. Yeats

A hundreth good pointes of husbandrie, Thomas Tusser

The Collected Works of Nathanael West: "The Day of the Locust", "The Dream Life of Balso Snell", "Miss Lonelyhearts", "A Cool Million", Nathanael West

Miss Lonelyhearts & The Day of the Locust, Nathaniel West

The Worst Journey in the World, Apsley Cherry-Garrard

Scott's Last Expedition, V1, R. F. Scott

The Herries Chronicle: Rogue Herries, Judith Paris, The Fortress and Vanessa, Hugh Walpole

Rogue Herries, Hugh Walpole

The Dream of Gerontius, John Henry Newman

The Brother of Daphne, Dornford Yates

The Poetry of Architecture: Or the Architecture of the Nations of Europe Considered in Its Association with Natural Scenery and National Character, John Ruskin

The Downfall of Robert Earl of Huntington, Anthony Munday

Gallathea, John Lyly

Clayhanger, Arnold Bennett

South: The Story of Shackleton's Last Expedition 1914-1917, Sir Ernest Shackketon

The Bishop and Other Stories, Anton Chekov

Greene's Groatsworth of Wit: Bought With a Million of Repentance, Robert Greene

Beau Sabreur, Percival Christopher Wren

The Hekatompathia, or Passionate Centurie of Love, Thomas Watson

 and many others

Tell us what you would love to see in print again, at affordable prices! Email: **benedictionbooks@btinternet.com**

Printed in Great Britain
by Amazon

58408808R00031